This book belongs to

....

Quarto is the authority on a wide range of topics.

Quarto educates, entertains and enriches the lives of our readers—enthusiasts and lovers of hands-on living.

www.quartoknows.com

© 2018 Quarto Publishing plc

First published in 2018 by QED Publishing,
an imprint of The Quarto Group.
The Old Brewery, 6 Blundell Street,
London N7 9BH, United Kingdom.
T (0)20 7700 6700 F (0)20 7700 8066
www.QuartoKnows.com

A catalogue record for this book is available from the British Library.

ISBN 978-1-78493-923-6

Based on the original story by Lucy Barnard
Author of adapted text: Katie Woolley
Series Editor: Joyce Bentley
Series Designer: Sarah Peden

Manufactured in Dongguan, China TL102017

9 8 7 6 5 4 3 2 1

MIX
Paper from
responsible sources
FSC® C104723

FSC
www.fsc.org

**Reading
Gems**

Watch Out, Ned!

Ned did not listen.

Watch out,
Ned!

Ned went down the long slide.

He had fun high up on the swing.

Ned went too fast on the roundabout.

Watch out, Ned!

Ned liked to jump over his bed.

But Ned liked
to climb up his
bookcase most
of all.

He had to climb up very high.

Ned was not scared when he fell down.

Ned did not listen to his teacher.

Ned went over to the river. He was
not scared.

But Ned wobbled and wobbled.

He fell all the way in! The river was very fast.

All the children went to help.

Help! Help!

17

Ned saw a
big waterfall.

It was a long
way down.

His friend got
a big stick.

The children
pulled and pulled.

Ned was safe.

When Ned did listen
he had the most fun of all.

Story Words

bed

bookcase

children

fell

friend

high

jump

Mum

Ned

river

roundabout

slide

stick

swing

teacher

waterfall

Let's Talk About Watch Out, Ned!

Look carefully at the front and back cover.

Ned and his friends are different animals.

How are they different?

How are they the same?

In the story, Ned does not listen to his mum or his teacher.

What happens when he does not listen?

Why is it important to listen to grown ups?

What do you think the water felt like when Ned fell in?

Was it hot or cold?

Ned's friends help him when he falls in the river.

Have you ever helped someone?

What has Ned learnt to do by the end of the story?

Fun and Games

Look at the pictures and read the sentences.
Is each sentence right or wrong?

His friend got a
big stick.

Ned liked to climb up
his bookcase.

Ned is in the river.

Ned did listen.

Look at the pictures, then look back at the story. Which picture is not in the story?

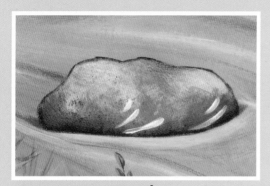

rock

picnic

cart

fish

bag

guitar

Answer: The cart is not in the story.

Your Turn

Now that you have read the story,
have a go at telling it in your own words.
Use the pictures below to help you.

GET TO KNOW READING GEMS

Reading Gems is a series of books that has been written for children who are learning to read. The books have been created in consultation with a literacy specialist.

The books fit into four levels, with each level getting more challenging as a child's confidence and reading ability grows. The simple text and fun illustrations provide gradual, structured practice of reading. Most importantly, these books are good stories that are fun to read!

Level 1 is for children who are taking their first steps into reading. Story themes and subjects are familiar to young children, and there is lots of repetition to build reading confidence.

Level 2 is for children who have taken their first reading steps and are becoming readers. Story themes are still familiar but sentences are a bit longer, as children begin to tackle more challenging vocabulary.

Level 3 is for children who are developing as readers. Stories and subjects are varied, and more descriptive words are introduced.

Level 4 is for readers who are rapidly growing in reading confidence and independence. There is less repetition on the page, broader themes are explored and plot lines straddle multiple pages.

Watch Out, Ned! follows an adventurous fox as he learns that listening is important. It explores themes of behaviour, friendship and safety.

Level 2

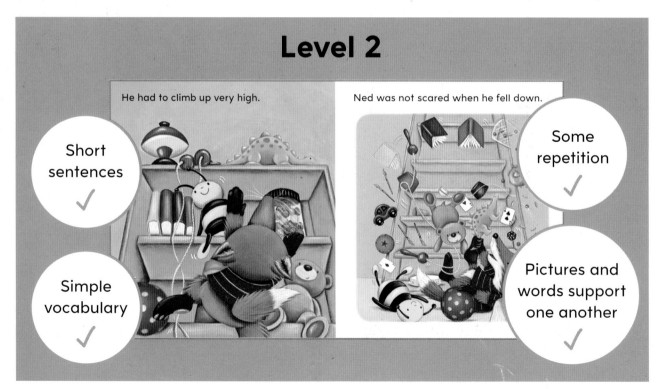

He had to climb up very high.

Ned was not scared when he fell down.

Short sentences ✓

Simple vocabulary ✓

Some repetition ✓

Pictures and words support one another ✓